PORCUPINE'S PIE

FOR ANDY, HENRY, AND NATHAN, WITH LOVE.
--L.R.

Text copyright © 2018 Laura Renauld
Illustrations copyright © 2018 Beaming Books

Published in 2018 by Beaming Books, an imprint of 1517 Media.
All rights reserved. No part of this book may be reproduced
without the written permission of the publisher.
Email copyright@1517.media.
Printed in the United States of America.
24 23 22 21 20 19 18   1 2 3 4 5 6 7 8

ISBN: 9781506431802

Written by Laura Renauld
Illustrated by Jennie Poh
Designed by Sarah DeYoung, Mighty Media, Inc.
Production by Alisha Lofgren, 1517 Media

Library of Congress Control Number:
2018942668

VN0004589; 9781506431802; SEPT2018

Beaming Books
510 Marquette Avenue
Minneapolis, MN 55402
beamingbooks.com

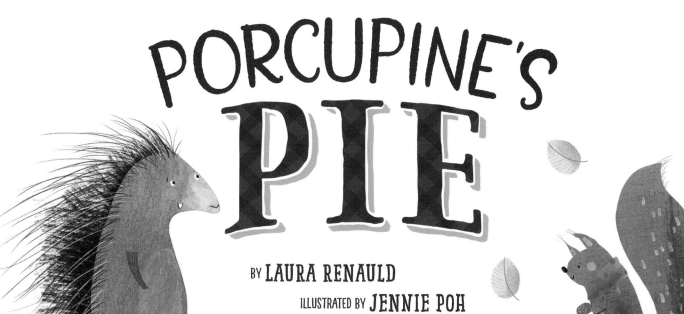

PORCUPINE'S PIE

BY **LAURA RENAULD**

ILLUSTRATED BY **JENNIE POH**

beaming books

MINNEAPOLIS

Porcupine prickled with excitement.
It was Fall Feast Day!

Her mouth watered as she opened her pantry:
one stick of butter, two handfuls of sugar, and
three scoops of flour. In a pail, she had a pile
of rosy, red cranberries. Just the right ingredients
to make her Famous Cranberry Pie.

Porcupine read her recipe.
"Step 1: Wash the cranberries."

She stepped into her favorite boots and
waddled down the path toward the river.

Porcupine stopped to rest at the
base of Squirrel's oak tree.
"Squirrel?" Porcupine called.
"Are you making your Famous
Nut Bread for Fall Feast Day?"

Squirrel poked her head out of her nest.
"No. It's just plain nuts for me this year.
Bread needs flour and I have none."

"Don't look so sad, Squirrel. I have flour to spare."

Squirrel scampered down the tree trunk.
"Really? Oh, THANK YOU, Porcupine!"

"The flour is in my pantry.
Help yourself."

Porcupine continued toward the river.
When she waddled by Bear's cave,
she called, "Bear? Are you making your
Famous Honey Cake for Fall Feast Day?"

Bear lifted his nose from a book.
"No. It's just plain honey for me this year.
Cakes need butter and I have none."

"Butter, you say? How much do you need?"

"Only half a stick."

"I have butter back in my den. Help yourself."

Bear dropped his book and nearly gave
Porcupine a hug. "THANK YOU, Porcupine!"

As Porcupine neared the river, Doe's thicket
came into view. "Doe?" Porcupine called.
"Are you making your Famous Apple Tart
for Fall Feast Day?"

Doe gracefully stepped out onto the trail.
"No. It's just plain apples for me this year.
Tarts need sugar and I have none."

"I'd be happy to lend you some sugar. Help yourself."

Doe's bright eyes widened. "Porcupine, THANK YOU!
You have made this a very special Fall Feast Day."

At the river, Porcupine looked inside her pail.
"Oh no!" she gasped. Her pail was empty.

Knock, knock, knock.
"Porcupine? Are you making your
Famous Cranberry Pie for Fall Feast Day?"

"No," Porcupine answered.
"It's just plain pie crust for me this year.
I lost my cranberries and now I have none."

She opened the door. Doe, Squirrel, and
Bear had their famous culinary creations
in one hand and an offering in the other.

"Leftover nuts," said Squirrel.
"A dribble of honey," said Bear.
"A few extra apples," said Doe.
"And a handful of cranberries," said Bear.

"I could just hug you," Porcupine beamed. "If I can't make my Famous Cranberry Pie, there's nothing better than a Festive *Friendship* Pie!"

FRIENDSHIP PIE

Invite your friends over to make your own Friendship Pie! Always ask an adult to join the fun (and help you with the stove).

INGREDIENTS

1 package refrigerated piecrust
1 cup cranberries, fresh or frozen
½ cup granulated sugar
1 tablespoon flour
¼ cup cranberry juice, or juice
   of your choice

¾ teaspoon cinnamon
4 apples, peeled and sliced
¼ cup sliced, toasted almonds,
   or nut of your choice
2 tablespoons honey
1 tablespoon butter

DIRECTIONS

1. Preheat oven to 425°F.

2. In a saucepan, combine the cranberries, sugar, flour, juice, and cinnamon. Cook over medium heat until bubbly and slightly thickened. Remove from heat and let cool.

3. In a large bowl, combine the apples, almonds, and honey. Stir to combine.

4. When the cranberry mixture is cool enough to touch, add it to the apple mixture. Stir to combine.

5. Line a 9-inch pie plate with one piecrust.

6. Pour the filling into the piecrust. Dot with butter and cover with the second crust.

7. Dip your finger in water and run it along the edge, between the piecrusts Press a fork around the edge to seal it.

8. Trim any excess dough. Cut a few slits in the top crust to allow steam to escape.

9. Bake for 35 to 45 minutes. It is done when the crust is brown and the filling is bubbling.

10. Cool, slice, and serve!

ABOUT THE AUTHOR

LAURA RENAULD is a former third-grade teacher. Laura grew up in Vermont, and now lives in northern Virginia with her husband and two sons. When she is not writing picture books, Laura can be found on a trail, at the library, or in the kitchen. On hikes near her home, Laura secretly hopes she will find a pie-baking porcupine.

ABOUT THE ILLUSTRATOR

JENNIE POH was born in England and grew up in Malaysia, in the jungle. At the age of ten, she moved back to England and went on to study Fine Art at the Surrey Institute of Art & Design, as well as Fashion Illustration at Central St Martins. Jennie loves the countryside, animals, tea and reading. She lives in Woking, England with her husband, two wonderful daughters, and two marmalade kittens.